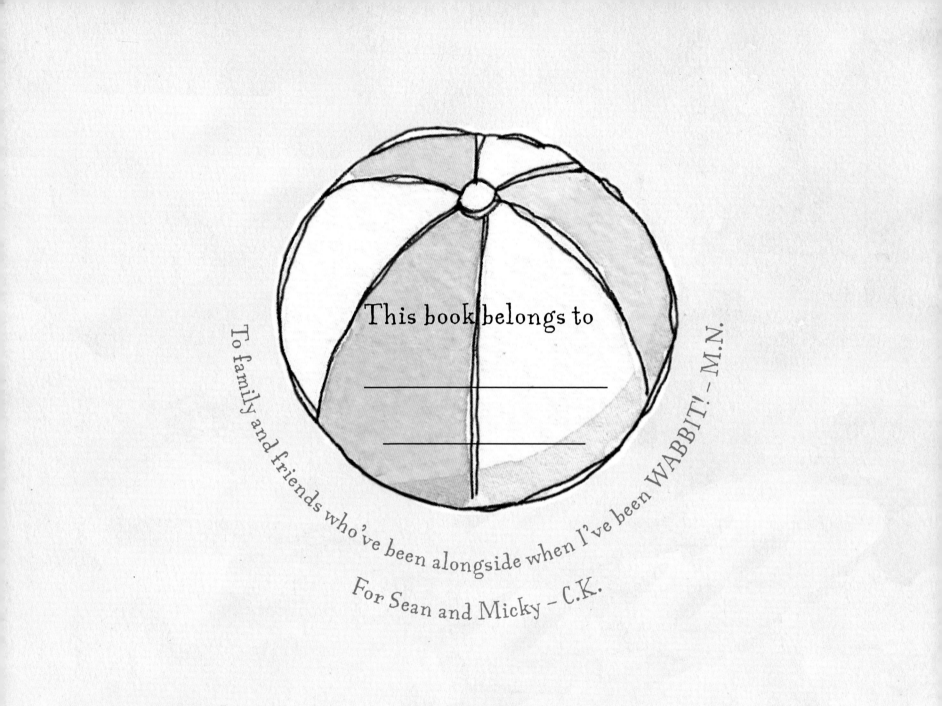

This book belongs to

_____

_____

To family and friends who've been alongside when I've been WABBIT! – M.N.

For Sean and Micky – C.K.

Picture Kelpies is an imprint of Floris Books. First published in 2014 by Floris Books. Text © 2014 Mike Nicholson. Illustrations © 2014 Claire Keay.
Mike Nicholson and Claire Keay assert their right under the Copyright, Designs and Patents Act 1988 to be recognised as the Author and Illustrator of this Work.
All rights reserved. No part of this book may be reproduced without prior permission of Floris Books, 15 Harrison Gardens, Edinburgh
www.florisbooks.co.uk
The publisher acknowledges subsidy from Creative Scotland towards the publication of this volume.
British Library CIP Data available
ISBN 978-178250-049-0 Printed in China

To Struan

Thistle Sands
A braw Scots story for bairns

Happy reading!

Mike Nicholson

Picture Kelpies

MIKE NICHOLSON
AND CLAIRE KEAY

It's a bright sunny day, let's go and explore,
Thistle Sands are just within reach.
Follow wee winding roads, hike through a field,
cross the dunes and you'll get to the beach.

People trek slowly with deck chairs and food;
Jamie zooms past them all on his scooter.
But he speeds from the path into sand and gets stuck,
and then it's a bit of a *fouter*.

Heather arrives for a swim at the beach,
and, like everyone, needs to get changed.
Some hide behind windbreaks or wrestle with towels,
getting their swimwear arranged.

Wasting no time, Heather pulls off her clothes,
there's no chance that she'll dilly-dally.
Her long legs flash white as she runs to the sea:
she's fast but she's so *peely-wally!*

Wee Archie stands watching the surfers,
determined that he'll have a shot.
He wants to ride waves with the big boys,
not paddle around like a tot.

"Just wait till you're older," his grandad advises.
"For surfing you need brains and brawn."
But Archie insists, and jumps on a board.
Grandad sighs, "That laddie is *thrawn!*"

Exploring the rock pools down by the cliffs,
Gregor discovers a cave.
It looks like a tunnel with no end in sight,
but holding his torch he feels brave.

He steps forward slowly... then gets a big fright:
there's a HOWL that's ghostly and spooky!
His cheeky friend Robbie leaps out from the dark,
making Gregor fall on his *bahookie*.

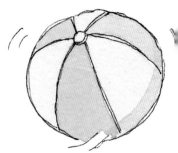

Ailsa and Duncan play with their beach ball,
bouncing it hard on the sand.

But the gathering breeze blows it high in the air.
Where is it going to land?

Agnes Auld's head is the place that gets hit.
She's so dazed that she has to shake it.

Poor Agnes was peacefully lost in a dream;
and now she looks totally *glaikit*.

The sandcastle contest is soon to be judged,
and Finlay is building with zest.
After hours spent digging and crafting,
he's certain that he'll beat the rest.

With windows, a drawbridge and towers, one, two, three,
he is proud of his fabulous palace.
But his flourish of planting a flag on the top
proves that Finlay has been a bit *gallus!*

At the back of the beach, the sand dunes are huge;
the wind and the waves make them grow.
The Docherty kids love to clamber up high
and slide down like they're sledging on snow.

But soft sandy slopes are terribly tiring
if exercise isn't your habit.
Their legs turn to jelly, they flop to the ground:
all that climbing has made them feel *wabbit*.

Caitlin has made the most beautiful shapes
by lining up shells on the sand.
She collected them first in her favourite pink bucket
then laid them out gently by hand.

But the tide's on the turn, with waves washing in,
heading straight for the patterns so neat.
As all of her shells are scattered away,
Caitlin sits down and has a good *greet*.

The children all hear a soft tinkle of music:
the tune from an ice-cream van.
They race up the beach, cross the dunes and the field
to get there as fast as they can.

It's Kirsty who's selling the cones, cans and sweets,
and tablet that's made by her granny.
Her dad serves the ice creams and she counts the change.
That's easy for Kirsty – she's *canny*.

Lachlan is paddling in rock pools,
poking around with his net.

He finds a big crab and a starfish,
and seaweed that's slimy and wet.

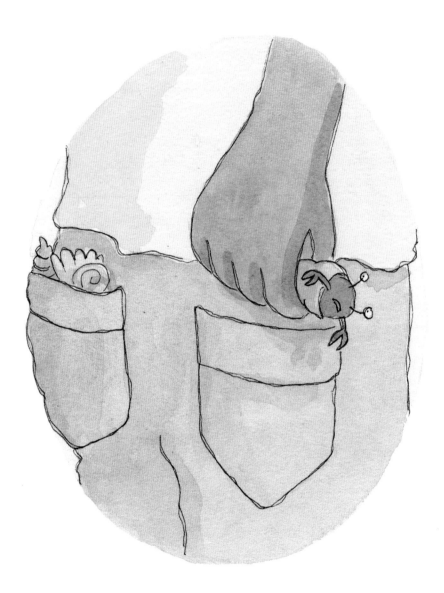

He picks out a few things he'd like to take home, and puts some wee shells in his pocket.

But a crab inside one of them gives him a nip. Lachlan slips – and ends up all *maukit*.

Mr Craig wakes to find himself buried.
All he can move are his eyes!
He'd only lain down to have forty winks;
this new sandy bed's a surprise.

"Was it you?" he bellows at Morag,
though he knows that she isn't the type.
"It was Struan!" She points to her brother.
He shouts back, "You're such a big *clype!*"

There's a cricket match on, some football as well,
and a volleyball game will soon start.
There's even a barefoot all-ages race
for those who still feel young at heart.

But Hector's dog, Shug, is after a ball;
he steals one and then does a runner.
His teeth are so sharp that it bursts with a POP!
For the footballers that's a real *scunner*.

The sky is now turning from blue to pale pink;
people wearily pack up their stuff.
For some the long walk up the dunes to the car
uses the last of their puff.

Mr Brodie feels fine; he takes big deep breaths,
piping everyone back with a skirl.
Agnes holds hands with Caitlin and Archie,
they finish the day with a *birl*.

Bahookie – bottom

Birl – spin in a dance

Canny – shrewd, clever

Clype – tell-tale

Fouter – a troublesome, fiddly task

Gallus – overly bold

Glaikit – daft looking

Greet – cry

Maukit – filthy

Peely-wally – pale

Scunner – disappointment, nuisance

Thrawn – stubborn

Wabbit – stunned, exhausted